# THE GIFT OF STORY

# The Gift of
# Story

## A WISE TALE ABOUT WHAT IS ENOUGH

*Clarissa Pinkola Estés, Ph.D.*

*Illustrations by Michael McCurdy*

BALLANTINE BOOKS

NEW YORK

Library of Congress Catalog Card Number: 93-90686
ISBN: 0-345-38835-6

TEXT DESIGN BY BETH TONDREAU DESIGN

Manufactured in the United States of America

First Edition: November 1993

10 9 8 7 6 5 4 3 2 1

To the old ones,
*a nagyszülőknek,*
*para los ancianos,*
the last of their kind.

# ALSO BY CLARISSA PINKOLA ESTÉS, PH.D.

## BOOKS*
*Women Who Run With the Wolves*

## AUDIO WORK[†]
*The Gift of Story:*
*On What Constitutes Enough*

*In the House of the Riddle Mother:*
*On Women's Archetypal Dreams*

*The Red Shoes:*
*On Torment and the Recovery of Soul Life*

*The Radiant Coat:*
*On the Crossing Between Life and Death*

*How to Love a Woman:*
*On Intimacy and the Erotic Life of Women*

*The Boy Who Married an Eagle:*
*On Male Individuation*

*The Wild Woman Archetype:*
*On the Instinctual Nature of Women*

*Warming the Stone Child:*
*On Abandonment and the Unmothered*

*The Creative Fire:*
*On the Cycles of Creative Life*

*\*Published by Ballantine Books*
*†Published by Sounds True, Boulder, Colorado*

# THE GIFT OF STORY

WITHIN THIS SMALL BOOK, THERE ARE several stories that, like Matrióchka dolls, fit one inside the other. Among my people, questions are often answered with stories. The first story almost always evokes another, which summons another, until the answer to the question has become several stories long. A sequence of tales is thought to offer broader and deeper insight than a single story alone. So, in this old tradition, let us begin with a question: What constitutes "enough"? Let me begin to answer by telling you a story.

This old tale was handed down to me in many different versions over many an evening fire. The tellers are various good and rustic people from Eastern Europe, most of whom still live by the oral tradition. The story is about the great wise man, the Bal Shem Tov.

The beloved Bal Shem Tov was dying and sent for his disciples. "I have acted as intermediary for you, and now when I am gone you must do this for yourselves. You know the place in the forest where I call to God? Stand there in that place and do the same. You know how to light the fire, and how to say the prayer. Do all of these and God will come."

After the Bal Shem Tov died, the first generation did exactly as he had instructed, and God always came. But by the second generation, the people had forgotten how to light the fire in the way the Bal Shem Tov had taught them. Nevertheless, they stood in the special place in the forest and they said the prayer, and God came.

By the third generation, the people had forgotten how to light the fire, and they had forgotten the place in the forest. But they spoke the prayer nevertheless, and God still came.

In the fourth generation, everyone had forgotten how to build the fire, and no one any longer knew just where in the forest one should stand, and finally, too, the prayer itself could not be recalled. But one person still remembered the story about it all, and told it aloud. And God still came.

As in this ancient story, as throughout all of human history, and in my deepest family traditions, the ultimate gift of story is twofold; that at least one soul remains who can tell the story, and that by the recounting of the tale, the greater forces of love, mercy, generosity and strength are continuously called into being in the world.

In both the traditions I come from, Mexican-Spanish by birth and immigrant Hungarian by adoption, the telling of story is considered an essential spiritual practice. Tales, legends, myths and folklore are learned, developed, numbered and preserved the way a pharmacopoeia is kept. A collection of cultural stories, and especially family stories, is considered as necessary for long and strong life as decent food, decent relationship and decent work. The life of a keeper of stories is a combination of researcher, healer, linguist in symbolic language, teller of stories, inspiratrice, God talker and time traveler.

In the apothecary of the hundreds of stories I was taught by both my families, most are not used as simple entertainment. In the folkloric application, rather, they are conceived of and handled as a large group of healing medicines, each requiring spiritual preparation and certain insights by the healer as well as by the subject. These medicinal stories are traditionally used in many different ways; to teach, correct errors, lighten, assist transformation, heal wounds, re-create memory. Their main purpose is to educate and enrich soul and worldly life.

It must be noted also that many of the most powerful medicines, that is stories, come about as a result of one person's or group's terrible and compelling suffering. For the truth is that much of the story comes from travail; theirs, ours, mine, yours, someone's we know, someone's we do not know far away in time and place. And yet, paradoxically, these very stories that rise from deep suffering can provide the most potent remedies for past, present and even future ills.

When I was a child, the few Hungarian family members who survived the devastating war in Europe found their way to America with help from those already here. Suddenly, I was the fortunate inheritor of additional extended family that included several remarkable old women. One in particular I called "Auntie Irena," which in Hungarian is an affectionate name for a storyteller, like the name "Mother Goose" in Britain and the United States. It was she who gave me a story about what "enough" really means.

She was then an old woman who became one of the treasures of my life for she was filled with an immense love for humans, and most especially for little children. Sometimes she awakened me in the mornings by shaking sprinkles of cold water on my face, and this she called her special blessing on me.

She rouged my cheeks with black cherry juice in the summertime. And once in the wintertime, and outside the bounds of propriety among adults in those times, she sledded with me down a hill and into a pasture, cackling all the way. Best of all, she knew innumerable stories. When I climbed into her lap, I felt I was sitting in a great warm throne, and all seemed right with us and with the world.

This was all the more extraordinary since she and this entire branch of the family had lived through years of unspeakable fear and inhumanity during the war. They were simple farm folk who lived in the tiny hamlets and remote villages. And like millions upon millions of kinsmen and kinswomen in countries throughout Europe, all were thrust into a war they did not make, yet were forced to endure or die. Auntie, like all who survived, repeated over and over again, "I cannot bear to speak of these things. No one can understand how terrible it was. No one can understand what it was like unless they saw it, smelled it, heard it, clung to life through it themselves." When I asked what

**6**

little present she would like for her birthday or for a holiday, her reply was always the same, "No gift please, *édes kis*, my sweet little one. The gifts I longed for are here now—to be able to hold a child again, to be able to feel love, to be able to laugh sometimes, and to finally be able, once more, to cry. All I have yearned for is here."

Here is the story she gave to me about "enough". She told the story in the third person, the way that people do when they "cannot bear to speak of these things". You may find the heart of the story familiar, for it is very old.

ong ago, during the war, a small farm in Hungary was overrun three times by three different armies. Toward the end of the war, in the winter just three days before Christmas, yet another army came, and took nearly everyone who was left away to forced labor camps. The others they marched to the border and left them there stripped of shoes and coats. By a miracle one of the old women was able to hide in the forest. Frightened and dejected, she wandered through the wood for endless hours, trying to make herself as black as a tree trunk one moment, as white as the snow the next. All about her was the starry night and from time to time, the sound of snow falling from the trees.

In time, she came to a small shed of the kind that hunters use. Finding it empty, she entered and sank to the floor in relief. It was only moments before she realized that there with her in the hut, half in shadow, was another soul. It was a very old man whose eyes were filled with fear. But she knew right away that he was not her enemy. In a moment he realized that she was not his either. To tell you the truth, they were both more odd looking than frightening. She wore men's pants that were too short, a coat with one sleeve missing, and an apron wrapped around her head for a hat.

As for him, his ears stuck out like this, and his hair was just two white tufts. His pants were like balloons with his two little twig legs inside them. His belt was so big it wound around his waist twice.

There they sat, two strangers with nothing to their names, stripped of everything except their own heartbeats. There they were, two refugees listening hard for footsteps in the snow, two souls ready to flee at a moment's notice. And together they carried all this heartbreak on a most beautiful night during which, in normal times, people everywhere would be celebrating in their own ways the high holiday season and the return of the blessed light to the world.

It was clear from the old man's way of speaking that he was far more learned than she. Even so, she was grateful when at last he said, "Let me tell a story to pass the night." Ah, a story, something familiar. In the times they lived, nothing, nothing, *nothing* made sense. But a simple story—*that* she could understand. This is the story he told...one that gave meaning to the question, "What is enough?" and made that night unlike any other before or since.

onight we have nothing," began the old man. "But somewhere in the world, no doubt, there are people who may have much more than they need. What is enough? Let us consider this question."

Once upon a time a long time ago, during the times our blessed grandparents were still living, there was a poor but beautiful young woman who was married to an equally poor but handsome young man. It was nearing the holiday time of year when gifts were customarily exchanged. The young people were very hard pressed, for a war that had raged over the land for many years had only recently receded.

All the sheep had been slaughtered by the soldiers for food. So, there was no wool to make thread. And without thread, there was no spinning, and without spinning, there was no cloth, and therefore no warm clothes to replace threadbare ones. As they were able, people cut up two pairs of shoes to make one pitiful pair. Everyone wore all the ragged sweaters and vests they owned, so that they looked deceptively robust in the belly, yet gaunt above and below.

Then, as often happens when the worst of war is over, people began to creep back to what was left of their homes. Like the dog that knows its own field, they came back to stay regardless of the poor conditions. Some of the farm women began to mend the plows, replacing the blades with shell casings they heated and shaped by hand. Others cut open and shook the dead plants searching for seed. The tailor begged a few scraps of cloth, and began to sew again and sell his patchwork vests and coats on the streets. The baker ground by hand whatever grain he could grow in broken pots in the window, then deftly shaped tiny breads which he sold from his front door. And gradually merchant-minded people began to gather a small living for themselves by selling little thises and thats—while thanking goodness that whatever evil war could do, it had not been able to blot out the sun. And so it went in the village. Though not bountiful, everywhere there reappeared the most simple signs of new life. And people took great care to protect all things that were either frail or young.

So it was that the beautiful young woman and the handsome young man lived. Though they had lost much in the war, they still had two fine possessions. He had managed to hold on to his grandfather's pocket watch, and was proud to tell the time to anyone who asked. And she, though ill-fed for months, still had beautiful long hair which, when she let it down, touched the ground all around her, covering her like a robe of finest sable. And so, rich in these simple ways, the young couple proceeded with their lives, eking pennies by selling a small turnip or winter apple here and there.

Oil and rag candles were lit in the windows

throughout the town for the holidays. The dark came earlier, stayed longer, and the snow flew fast. The young woman wanted so much to give her dear husband a gift for the holiday, a big bright beautiful gift. However, when she searched her pockets, she found only a few pennies. And as she considered her plight without even the smallest amount of self-pity, she still could not help but silently weep.

She realized that tears would not help if a gift for her loved one was still to be found, so she dried her cheeks, and plotted a plan. She pulled on her worn coat, and two pairs of gloves, each with different fingers missing. Out the door and down the muddy street she ran, past all the little shops with not so much in their windows. Now nothing else mattered for she had in mind a gift, a special gift for her husband who worked so hard and toiled so long to bring home what little he could.

Past piles of rubble, past stairs with no houses behind them, and down a narrow alley she ran, and then into a drab building. Up three flights of stairs she ran, by then breathless, and with barely strength enough to knock at the door.

Madame Sophie answered, wearing a miserable moth-eaten little mink around her throat. Her hair was orange and stuck out all over her head. Her eyebrows were like sooty scrub brushes. Surely she was the oddest old woman who ever walked the face of the earth. She, who before the war had made fine wigs for wealthy men and women, was now reduced to living in a one room flat with no heat.

Madame Sophie's eyes glittered. "Ah, have you come to sell your hair?" she cooed.

She and the young woman bickered back and forth until at last a deal was struck. The young woman sat in the wooden chair. Madame Sophie lifted one of the young woman's heavy tresses to the light. It shined like silken floss. With shears the size, it seemed, of great black iron jaws, Madame Sophie cut the young woman's glorious locks right off in three great snips. The lovely shanks of hair fell to the floor, and the young woman's sparkling tears fell with them. Madame Sophie gathered the shorn hair together as if she were a greedy rodent.

"Here's your money," the old woman barked. She dropped some coins into the young woman's hand, pushed her out into the hall and slammed the door shut.

And that was that.

Despite suffering such an ordeal, the young woman was guided by her inner vision, and her eyes lit with enthusiasm once again. She rushed down the street to a man who was selling watch chains made of lead covered in silvery tin—but assuredly looking finer than a simple string any day. She gave to him the several pennies she had before and those she had earned from selling her beautiful hair. And with grimy hands he handed her a watch chain. Oh, how suddenly filled with joy she was to have a gift to give to her beloved. Why she fairly ran home, her feet barely touching the ground like the angel that she, in another time and place, might certainly have been.

All the while, her husband was busy at his own work of finding a gift for his dear one. Oh what could it be? What would be just right? A vendor thrust a shriveled potato toward him. No, no, that would not do. Another vendor held out a scarf, that though bedraggled, was a pretty color. But no, it would cover her lovely hair, and he so liked to see her hair with its glints of ruby and gold.

On the next windy corner, yet another vendor held out in his palms two plain and simple combs; one was perfect, the other had only one broken tooth. The young man knew he had found the perfect gift.

"Twelve pennies for these fine combs?" wheedled the man.

"But I do not have twelve pennies," said the young man.

"Well, what do you have?" whined the man. And the barter began.

Meanwhile, back in their tiny rented room, the young woman moistened her hair with a little water and coaxed it to curl around her face and then sat awaiting her husband. "Let him think I am still lovely in my own way," she whispered in silent prayer. Soon she heard his steps on the stair. In he rushed, poor soul, rail thin, red nosed, icy fingered, but with all the earnestness and hope of the newly born. And there on the door sill, he stopped in his tracks, staring at his wife quite dumbfounded.

"Oh, do you not like my hair, dear husband? Do you not like it? Well, please say something. To tell you the truth, I cut it so that a good could come from it for your sake. Please say something my love."

The young man was torn between pain and laughter, but mirth overtook him at last. "My dearest," he said and held her close. "Here I have your gift for this holiday season." Out from his pocket he drew the combs. For a moment her face grew brighter, and then all her features plummeted downward as she burst into tears and fairly howled with woe.

"My love," he comforted, "your hair shall grow back some day, and these combs will be glorious then. Let us not be sad."

All right then, she straightened herself. Her happiness returned as she brought out the gift she had for him. "Here, this is your gift my dear husband." And in her palm lay the simple chain, her gift of sacrifice for him.

"Ha!" he hooted, jumped up, and began to pace the floor. "Do you know I sold my watch to buy your combs?"

"You did? You did?" she cried.

"I did! I did!" he cried.

They hugged and laughed and cried together, and promised one another that the future would be better, it would, truly it would, just wait and see.

So, you see, though some might say these two young people were foolish and unwise, they were in fact, like the magi who sought the messiah. Even though the magi with righteous intention brought gifts of gold, frankincense and myrrh, in the end, that which they carried within their hearts had the most value, their yearning and devotion.

And the young couple here, like the magi, were wise too, for they gave the most golden of all things possible. They gave their love, their truest love to one another.

And it was enough.

nd with this, the old man, who was hardly more than a heap of bones, ended his story. There in the hut, his words made the loneliness and fear each of them felt, less lonely, less fearsome. Not because reason to fear was lifted magically from them, for it was not, but because the story provided them with strength.

There they sat, the old man and the old woman, on that evening of the holiday time. He revealed to her that it was near the time of Chanukah, the time of year he and his loved ones normally gave *gelt,* small gifts of coins. And she told him it was somewhere near Christmas, a time of year during which her people also exchanged gifts.

And they smiled sadly, for both their traditions required gifts and there they were with absolutely nothing to give anyone. They sat in silence, until suddenly these words leapt out of the old woman's heart.

"I know. I will give you the gift of the sky above us."

And she could see that something swept through his heart, for he closed his eyes for a long moment, inhaled deeply, then opened his eyes again, and looked directly at her. He replied, "I am honored to receive your gift to me." And the old woman expected him to say no more.

Then all of a sudden he spoke again. "And...and I give you in return, the gift of these stars overhead."

"Also I am honored," she said. And they sat on in mutual heartache, a deepening joy, and contemplation.

Words rushed again into her mouth, from where she did not know. "And I return the favor to you, for I will give you the...the gift of the moon this night."

He remained silent for a long, long time. He was searching the sky for something else to give, but there was nothing left, for they had given everything that could be seen in the night sky. So they sat in utter quiet.

At last the words came to him. "Ah, I see it now. I return your kindness by giving you the story that I have just told. Keep it safe. Carry it out of these woods in great health."

And they nodded, for they knew that a strong story, perhaps more than anything else, could light the dark fields and forests that lay ahead for each.

In that hut, on that night, in that wood, they dared to recall their pasts; times of laughter, candle-light, steaming food, friendly faces, arms about their shoulders, the music of fiddles, the dancing and rosy-faced children. They drew on the warmth of the gifts given, certain for that time at least, and perhaps forever, that there was reason to believe in the ultimate goodness of humans.

Perhaps it was the apron she gave to him to cover his poor head, for like the young woman in his tale, the old woman had far more hair than the old man. Or perhaps it was because the stars and the moon had become their great timepiece, like the watch of the young man in the tale. Or maybe because the trails they would follow lay before them like a silvery watch chain, or perhaps because they might someday be able to look forward to the growing back of something of theirs that once was beautiful and unencumbered. Whatever the reasons, and maybe for a thousand reasons that they could not, that you and I cannot, nor any of us will ever completely understand...but blessed be that it was so, because...

it was enough.

According to my dear aunt, the old man and old woman both agreed that it was safer to go forth separately. So, the following evening in a wintry twilight in Hungary, they parted and went their ways, taking their chances alone in the forest. Like so many others in a war devastated land, their fates became God's business. And that is all we know, for they never saw one another again.

As a child, I wanted to search for them and confirm their survival. "What became of them, where can they be?" I asked. Auntie explained that the old man was really a special kind of being, one who could perhaps never die, for surely his stories kept him strong and alive, as the stories she knew kept her alive, and as mine would do for me. "And the old woman?" I asked. "Where can she be?"

Silence. Then, looking into the distance to a place only she could see, Auntie said, "I believe she may yet be living."

# EPILOGUE

I HAVE HEARD MANY ORAL VERSIONS OF the old man's story, and as a young adult, I read one similar to his called "Gifts of the Magi," authored by O. Henry in 1905. I am still taken with how the core of story remains the same stalwart, glowing thing, regardless of what ornamentation or variant words are placed around it.

In the oral tradition, "Gifts of the Magi" is called a literary story, which is usually a short story written down using elements culled from or clearly reminiscent of much older folktales. It is possible that the old man's story was derived from the literary tale. It may have been mixed with themes from old eastern European fairy tales. "Purchasing the wonderful object that becomes useless" is a common leitmotif in the old tales, generally revolving around the selling or bartering of one item in order to purchase another, but having the new item become utterly useless because of the unforeseen actions of another person or force. Sometimes there is an additional twist; inexplicably or by virtue of a change in consciousness or perspective, the useless thing becomes useful again. The Jack and the Beanstalk tale is an example of this.

Worldwide there are many ancient stories that revolve around the idea of bitter but instructive irony. While some deal in trivial irony, others treat issues of life and death. The story "Wolfen" or "Gellert" is about a man who slays his faithful dog because he thinks it has killed his infant child. Shortly after, the man discovers that his dog had slain a wolf in order to protect his child, who was still safe. In "The Pearl" by John Steinbeck, a poor man and woman win one treasure, a pearl, while losing another, their child. Many of the plays and poems of Federico García Lorca are masterpieces of bitter irony, as are many of the plays of Henrik Ibsen.

However, the old man's and my aunt's story, though both bitterly ironic in their own ways, also contain an additional heartening twist—that love can prevail over losses. Even after all these years since my aunt suffered a stroke and slowly slipped away from our family circle, I continue to feel a profound love and gratitude to her, and also to the stranger in the hut in the woods who strengthened someone I loved, who in turn strengthened me, so I could tell you about the gift of story, and so you can be encouraged to offer the gift of your own stories to others whom you care for.

In this way, you see that story as gift has generativity, and genealogy. Already, just by your reading my words, we have come to the fifth generation of the story about the young man and young woman who sold their valuables, gaining items that became useless, but which caused them to return to their ground note, the greater treasure of their love for one another.

Someone told the old man,

the old man told my aunt,

my aunt told me,

I told you,

perhaps you will tell another,

and the other might tell another too.

For some stories, considerations about the right time, right place, right person, right preparation and right purpose guides when and whether the story should be told or not. But for family stories, stories from one's culture and stories from one's personal life, anytime may be just the right time to give the gift of story.

Like night dreams, stories often use symbolic language, therefore bypassing the ego and persona, and traveling straight to the spirit and soul who listen for the ancient and universal instructions imbedded there. Because of this process, stories can teach, correct errors, lighten the heart and the darkness, provide psychic shelter, assist transformation and heal wounds.

In our present time, there is a goodness to, and a necessity for, rugged independence among individuals. But this is often best served and supported in good measure by deliberate interdependence with a community of other souls. Some say that community is based on blood ties, sometimes dictated by choice, sometimes by necessity. And while this is quite true, the immeasurably stronger gravitational field that holds a group together are their stories…the common and simple ones they share with one another.

Though these may revolve around crises tamed, tragedy averted, death be not denied, help arriving at the last moment, foolish undertakings, hilarity unbounded and so on—the tales people tell one another weave a strong fabric that can warm the coldest emotional or spiritual nights. So the stories that rise up out of the group become, over time, both extremely personal and quite eternal, for they take on a life of their own when told over and over again.

Whether you are an old family, a new family or a family in the making, whether you be lover or friend, it is the experiences you share with others and the stories that you tell about those experiences afterward, and the tales you bring from the past and future that create the ultimate bond.

There is no right or wrong way to tell a story. Perhaps you will forget the beginning, or the middle or the end. But a little piece of sunrise through a small window can lift the heart regardless. So cajole the old grumpy ones to tell their best memories. Ask the little ones their happiest moments. Ask the teenagers the scariest times of their lives. Give the old ones the floor. Go all around the circle. Coax out the introverts. Ask each person. You will see. Everyone will be warmed, sustained by the circle of stories you create together.

Though none of us will live forever, the stories can. As long as one soul remains who can tell the story, and that by the recounting of the tale, the greater forces of love, mercy, generosity and strength are continuously called into being in the world, I promise you…

it will be enough.

# ABOUT THE AUTHOR

CLARISSA PINKOLA ESTÉS, PH.D., IS AN AWARD-winning poet, a certified Jungian psychoanalyst, and a *cantadora* (keeper of the old stories) in the Latina tradition. She has been in private practice for twenty years, and is former executive director of the C.G. Jung Center in Colorado. Her book, *Women Who Run With the Wolves*, a compendium of twenty fairy tales and their interpretive and psychological applications to the inner life, has been hailed as a classic and as the seminal work on the instinctive nature of women. Dr. Estés heads the nascent Guadelupe Foundation, which has as one of its missions to broadcast strengthening stories—via short-wave radio—to various trouble spots throughout the world. She is the author of a nine volume audio series using story and psychoanalytic commentary, the latest being *How to Love a Woman: On Intimacy and the Erotic Life of Women*. Her next book, on the archetype of the wise old woman in fairy tales, and the curiously special gifts she has to offer to women of all ages, will be published by Ballantine in 1994.